Count your Blessings

Written by Kimberly Redway

Illustrated by Derren Toussaint

Collins

Chapter 1

Our class was travelling on an ancient coach to the museum. As it shuddered along the road, something caught in my hair. I felt for what it was. A hairband. I looked up as Jennings bounded down the aisle to me, her jumbo braids hanging over her shoulders. As she held a hand out for the hairband, a chunky bracelet slid down her arm. She had a beauty spot on the back of her hand. Her boots were expensive – I knew this because I'd seen them in the shop and asked my mum for them.

Next to her, I looked like a little kid. My hair was up in high bunches and I was small and slight. Jennings liked to line her eyes with a kohl pencil. My mum wouldn't let me wear make-up to school. I was about to hand the hairband back to her when Ms Dana turned around.

"Jennings, sit down," she said wearily.

Jennings shrugged and made her way back to sit with Ruby, my once best friend.

The museum had an art gallery full of stunning paintings. I'd been there a lot, using them as inspiration for my drawings. I loved the peace inside – often the only sound was the clop of many shoes moving from exhibit to exhibit. But today I wasn't excited. All I wanted was to talk to Ruby, who had her head close to Jennings. I was near enough that I could hear them talking.

"I finally got a dog," Ruby said. "You should come see him."

"Sure," Jennings said.

I remembered the first day Jennings came into my life. She'd been new at school, and Ms Dana had said, "I need a volunteer to show Jennings around."

Ruby's hand had shot up. I'd blinked at her, unsure of Jennings as she'd stood at the front of the class with a hand on her hip. She'd had a look of slight amusement on her face.

"OK, Ruby and Kirsten," Ms Dana had said. "Jennings, please sit with them."

Jennings had American sweets in her bag that she'd shared with me and Ruby at breaktime.

"They call sweets 'candy' over there," Jennings had said. "I know that because I went to New York last month – it was so awesome."

We'd hung out for the next two weeks.

All the while, Jennings had told us about her hamster Eddie, her cool older sister Lily who gave her make-up, and her life in London.

"At my last birthday party, we had a DJ," Jennings had said, grinning. "My mum gave out these huge goodie bags with expensive charm bracelets, candy and mobile phones."

Until last week, I'd trailed behind the two of them. I'd listened to Jennings talk and Ruby agree, but then last Monday everything had changed.

"That film was so cool, right?" Jennings had asked Ruby, who suddenly looked sheepish.

"What film?" I'd asked Ruby.

"We went to the cinema yesterday," Ruby said, looking at her shoes.

After that, they'd started leaving me out.

"There isn't much space with us," Jennings had said, at lunchtime. "You could sit next to Maisie instead ... "

When we'd had independent study, Ruby and Jennings sat together. At breaktimes, they'd disappeared before I could catch them up and then sat giggling in the corner of the playground.

The coach finally stopped outside the museum and Ms Dana stood up. She clapped her hands together.

"We're going to go into the museum now," she said. "I expect world-class behaviour. Is that understood?"

Did she think we were five?

We all nodded and answered, "Yes," walking into the large, cool building away from the beating sun. Inside the foyer, there was a large statue of a man bending over and pointing to the entrance of the museum. Ms Dana handed out clipboards with worksheets attached.

"I've been to this huge museum in London," Jennings said to Ruby, "with dinosaur models and dummies wearing Victorian clothes. This one is – " She put her thumb down.

I ignored Jennings and started working through the questions on the clipboard, wandering around the museum by myself. After about an hour, I walked into a room with a gigantic painting of a fountain. I read its description.

"The Fountain of Wishes was created in 1952 and is designed to accept coins that make your dreams come true. Throw one in and prepare to be amazed at the turn your life will take. The legend goes that explorer Gregory Hamilton found the fountain of youth in Jamaica. Its water was said to keep you young, so he took some home and built the Fountain of Wishes, filling it with this water."

Jennings came over with Ruby and they looked at
the description too.

"That's so uncool. Who believes in such things?" Jennings
said, looking at me as if I was the uncool person. "Come on,
Ruby, it's lunchtime."

Everyone followed Ms Dana outside, and there it was –
huge and made of white stone. Coins glinted at the bottom just
under the water.

"We'll have lunch out here," Ms Dana said. As we sat
on the picnic benches, I screwed up my face at the thought
of my lunch. Cheese sandwich, apple juice – it was so basic.
I could see Jennings had sushi.

I ate while staring at the fountain. The shimmering water splashed down into a large pool with coins scattered at the bottom. I pulled a coin out of my purse. Mum had given me money for the gift shop.

"I want to be Jennings. I want to be cool," I thought, before throwing the coin into the fountain. I closed my eyes and put my fingers to my mouth. It was still my slim one, nothing like Jennings' big, full lips. I wanted her sparkling eyes and pointed chin too.

After lunch, we did a history quiz until it was time to go home.

"That was so boring," I heard Jennings say on the coach, and Ruby nodded. "At my last school, we went to a theme park – "

I put my earphones in and slumped down in my seat. Everything Jennings did was cool and I really didn't want to hear any more.

I walked home by myself. When I opened the front door, Mum greeted me with a grin.

"How was it?" she asked. She had a smudge of paint on her cheek and her hair was up in a knot.

I just nodded.

"Are you OK, Kirsten?" Mum asked. "You seem really down."

"Ruby only wants to hang out with Jennings now,"
I said. "She's so cool, Mum. And she's been to so many
amazing places. I … I wish I was like her."

"I know it might seem like Jennings' life is perfect,"
Mum said. "But I'm sure if you walked a day in her shoes,
you'd see that everyone has problems."

I sighed and didn't say anything else. Dinner was ackee and
saltfish, and afterwards we played a board game.

When I started yawning, Dad said, "Bedtime, kid."

I got ready for bed, snuggled down under my quilt and
fell asleep.

✳ ✳ ✳

When I woke up the next morning, for a moment I was unsure of what I was seeing. The bedroom walls were yellow, with large posters of pop stars. I looked down at my hands – they seemed bigger and my right hand had a beauty spot on the back. Panic swept over me.

I scrambled out of bed towards a full-length mirror. I looked at myself and screamed.

These weren't my long arms. My high bunches were gone, and I was suddenly so much taller. The reflection staring back at me wasn't mine, but Jennings'.

Chapter 2

"What's all this noise?" Jennings' mum asked, coming into the bedroom. She was tottering about on really high heels and wearing a navy suit with a white blouse. "Jennings, you aren't dressed."

I could only stare at myself. So this was what it was like to be tall. This was ... terrifying.

"Sorry, Mrs Jones," I managed to say, as I looked at the pink pyjamas I was wearing.

"Jennings, I'm not in the mood for any of this ... nonsense," she said, eyes narrowed, hands on hips. "I am and always have been 'Mum'."

"Sorry ... Mum," I said, trying it out. The words sounded so strange coming from my mouth.

"What's going on?" asked Jennings' 13-year-old sister Lily, walking into the room now too. Her face was coated in a thick green mud mask and she had a white dressing gown wrapped around her.

"Just Jennings," Jennings' mum said, as if that explained everything.

"You are so annoying," Lily said, before stomping out.

My heart was leaping about in panic, but I knew I had to pretend to be Jennings. I took a deep breath and twitched a little. Who'd believe we'd swapped bodies?

I tried to grin and turned to Jennings' mum. "I'm just warming up my singing voice," I said, to explain my scream. I'd heard Jennings say that during PE once.

"I don't have time to mess about," Mrs Jones said, leaving the room. "Get ready, please."

I looked around the bedroom. Jennings had a huge TV on the wall, and a laptop open on her desk. I opened the wardrobe, which was packed with different clothes. She had dresses with sequins, tops with huge slogans and at least three pairs of ripped jeans. It'd happened. I was Jennings. This was nuts!

Shaking, I picked out a pair of grey jeans and a T-shirt with "Whatever!" written on the front. I walked out into the hallway and bumped into Lily.

"Why do you look so ... happy?" she asked, her eyes narrowed.

"Because it's Saturday," I said. "No school, right?" I put my hand on my hip like Jennings would.

Lily pulled a face and rolled her eyes. "You really are annoying," she said, before walking off.

I found the bathroom, had a shower and got changed. Just as I'd got back to the bedroom, Jennings' mum walked in, searching through her handbag. She stopped, looked at me and glared. "What are you wearing?" she asked.

"Clothes?" I said, because that was so Jennings.

"You're going to your nan's today while I'm at work, and you know she prefers you to wear a dress." She flung open the wardrobe doors and rifled through the clothes, pulling out a floral monstrosity covered with ruffles. "After what you did, you want to make sure you please her."

I changed in silence, wondering what Mrs Jones had meant. When I walked down the stairs, Lily burst out laughing.

"You look like a doll, and not in a good way," she said.

"There's a good way to look like a doll?" I asked.

Lily narrowed her eyes.

Wait ... I was meant to be Jennings. That hadn't sounded like her. "I mean ... who even cares?" I said. That was better.

"Clearly you do," Lily said, shrugging.

Mrs Jones herded me out of the door. Lily was wearing huge sunglasses and ripped jeans, with her hair in really long twists.

"Don't you have to wear a dress too?" I asked her.

"Why would I? I'm older," Lily said. "Besides, you're lucky Nan is even talking to you right now."

"What do you mean?"

"You know! Letting Eddie loose in Nan's house. We still can't find him, thanks to you."

So Eddie was lost. Jennings hadn't said anything.

Mrs Jones drove us to a bungalow a few minutes away. Everything inside was coated in dust – the curtains, the ornaments over the fireplace, even the cushions. Jennings' nan sat in a plump pink armchair, peering through gold-rimmed glasses, as she knitted something. She looked up at me and scowled.

I rushed over to hug her. Was that what Jennings would do? Jennings' nan held her hand up.

"Don't come near me after the fiasco with that rat," she said.

"It was a hamster, Mum," Mrs Jones said.

"Rat, hamster," Jennings' nan replied. "Same thing."

"Get out your homework, girls," Mrs Jones said to us.

"Um ... I didn't bring mine," I said.

Mrs Jones turned around slowly to me. "If you continue like this, you'll be on punishment," she said. "No TV, and no laptop except for homework. All this acting out is getting ridiculous."

She looked at me, waiting for an answer. What would Jennings say? I wasn't sure, so I said what Kirsten would say instead. "Sorry ... Mum."

"Right ... OK," Mrs Jones said, peering at me. "I'm off now. Be good for your nan."

She rushed out of the room and the front door slammed.

"I'll get you two some toast," Jennings' nan said,
shuffling off. Lily pulled exercise books out of her satchel.

"What can I do?" I asked.

"Find something," Lily said. "I'm not your babysitter."

"Can I have some paper?" I asked.

"What for?" she said, screwing up her nose.

"I want to draw something."

"Well, if you want to embarrass yourself. Here."

Jennings' nan came back with toast. It was really hard, but at least it wasn't burnt. I sat cross-legged on the carpet and started sketching Lily as she bent over her books at the table.

"Wait, is that me?" she asked, looking over. "Who even are you?"

"Jennings, of course," I said, pulling a face.

"Duh!" she said and went back to her homework.

We continued in silence for a couple of hours. Eventually Jennings' nan put down her knitting again and announced, "I'll make soup."

Lily sighed. "Not the soup ... anything but that," she whispered.

Jennings' nan returned with bowls of mushroom soup. It was far too salty.

"I'm not hungry," Lily said, pushing the soup away.

"Yeah, neither am I," I said.

"Eat it all, both of you," their nan snapped.

I sighed and began eating quickly so I couldn't taste it. I looked at Lily. She was taking the tiniest of sips while watching me with narrowed eyes. She suddenly grabbed my arm and pulled me out of the living room into the kitchen.

Lily stared into my eyes and said, "You're not Jennings!"

Chapter 3

"No ... I'm not," I said. How had she figured it out so quickly?

Lily burst out laughing. "I'm just messing with you ... You should have seen your face. But why are you acting so weird, eating Nan's soup ... drawing like you actually have talent? You're not even arguing with me."

Was I doing a good impression of Jennings? It didn't feel like it. I felt like I was wearing shoes the wrong size – like *everything* was wrong. I sighed. It would be a relief to tell the truth.

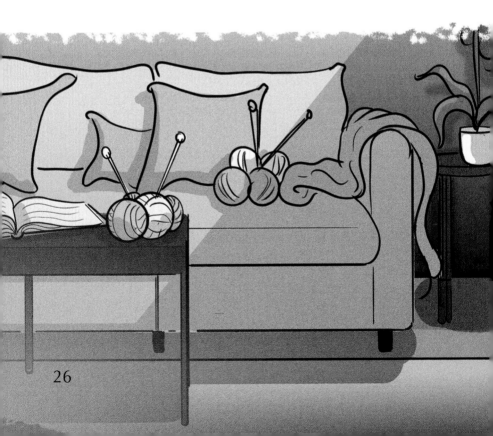

I took a deep breath. "That's because I'm not Jennings."

"OK, ha ha, joke's over," Lily said.

"Seriously. I made a wish in the Fountain of Wishes and now I'm in her body!"

Lily searched my face and then she laughed again. "You're so funny. Come on, let's watch YouTube. Nan's probably asleep by now."

I wasn't sure whether to be pleased Lily thought I passed as Jennings or annoyed she didn't believe me.

She pulled her laptop out of her bag and we watched some videos of older girls showing off their clothing hauls.

"Do you want to play a game?" I asked her, getting a bit bored. I'd spotted a pack of Pairs cards sitting on the worktop.

"You and me?" she asked.

"Yes, you and me." I began shuffling the Pairs cards the way Dad had shown me.

"Who taught you that?" Lily asked in awe.

I shrugged. She wouldn't believe the truth. As we played, Lily started to relax. We watched more YouTube and before we knew it, the doorbell went – Mrs Jones had arrived to collect us.

"Did you find Eddie?" Jennings' mum asked, as she drove home.

"Um … no," I said. With everything else, I'd completely forgotten about the missing hamster.

She shook her head and sighed.

When we got back, Lily grabbed my hand and pulled me up the stairs into her bedroom. It was painted purple with a collage of photos covering one wall.

"OK, I need you to sit down and tell me what's going on," Lily said.

I sat on the edge of her bed and peered up at her. "What do you mean?"

"Being nice all day," she said. "Playing cards with me, not arguing. What do you want? I'm not lending my new bag to you so –"

"I don't want to borrow your new bag," I said.

"OK, that confirms it, you're so not Jennings."

I was about to argue, to pretend to be Jennings, but the truth was ... this was exhausting. And I was worrying what Jennings was doing in my body. Was she reading my diary? Was she arguing with my mum? What were my family thinking?

"You're right. I'm Kirsten," I said.

Lily sucked in a breath, her eyes wide. "So you were telling the truth with the fountain thing? And I thought maybe Jennings was being nice for once ... "

"I ... want to go home," I said, thinking of my mum and dad.

"But you just got here," Lily said, sitting on the bed beside me.

"I know but ... nothing is what I thought it'd be."

Lily put an arm around me.

"Well, you'll see Jennings on Monday at school, right?" she said. "Then you can switch back. There must be some way to do it."

I nodded but my insides felt heavy at the thought of having to pretend for another day.

Sunday was even worse than Saturday. For lunch, Jennings'
nan served a tough piece of meat that was hard to chew and
tasted like wood. I did Jennings' homework, but it wasn't
the same without Dad helping me. I remembered to look for
Eddie, but I couldn't find him anywhere in the dusty house.
I even searched the kitchen cupboards, but they were filled
with more tins of terrible soup.

Mrs Jones didn't arrive to collect us until after dinner.
I went to the bathroom quickly before the trip home. I gasped
when I saw a shirt on the tiled floor moving slowly. I walked
over to it and picked it up. Underneath it was ... a hamster.

"You must be Eddie!" I said, picking him up.

I brought him into the living room and Jennings'
nan yelped. "Get that rat away from here!"

Mrs Jones pulled a face. "At least you've found him,"
she sighed.

"Sleepover?" Lily asked back home, as I put Eddie back in
his cage.

I nodded and we climbed into her bunk bed – Lily on
the top bunk and me on the bottom.

"Thanks for hanging out with me," I said.

"What are big sisters for?" Lily said, grinning as she peered down at me. "And maybe tomorrow you'll get your body back."

I fell asleep with that thought in my mind. I wanted it so much – but I didn't even know how we'd do it. Worrying, I tossed, turned and tangled myself in my blanket. When I woke the next morning, it felt as if I'd only slept for half an hour.

Jennings' mum put a cereal box in front of me when I came downstairs. She was brushing her hair, sliding pins in to hold it in place.

The cereal flakes looked like cardboard and tasted about the same. But it didn't matter. Today was the day. I just needed to talk to Jennings and work out how we'd switch back.

Lily hugged me before we got in the car. "You have to visit us when you're Kirsten again," she said.

"Sure," I said, grinning.

✳ ✳ ✳

At school, Jennings was sitting on a bench by herself. I walked over to her, but Ruby intercepted me.

"Hey, Jennings," Ruby said. "I wanted to go to the cinema with you at the weekend, but your mum said to wait until a weekday. She said you were busy visiting your nan."

"Ruby, I just need to talk to Jennings ... I mean, Kirsten," I said. "I'll only be a minute."

Ruby looked surprised, but she let me go.

Jennings looked up as I approached.

"I need to talk to you," I said. "We need to switch back. I know I made the wish, but I want my life back."

"Wait, you made the wish?"

"Well ... yeah."

"Thank you! Your parents rock — they spent most of the weekend with me and we even went to the zoo. I mean totally babyish, but who can resist the giraffes? And your mum's teaching me to sew."

"Oh cool. But we need to swap back now."

"I don't want to swap back."

Chapter 4

I blinked at Jennings, waiting for her to laugh and tell me how uncool I was. I waited for her to tell me my life was a snoozefest and she couldn't wait to be her again.

"But I found Eddie," I said, so stunned it was the only thing I could think to say.

"That old rat," Jennings said, waving a hand. "I wanted a dog like Ruby's. Not a hamster. My mum never listens. Why would I want to go back?"

"But your parents throw you expensive parties," I said. "And you've been to America."

Jennings shrugged. "So what?"

"But, Jennings –"

"You made the wish to switch. Tough luck."

"So, cinema tomorrow?" Ruby asked, coming up behind me. She slipped her arm through mine.

"I'd better go inside," Jennings said.

She walked off and I turned to Ruby. "Why were you talking to Kirsten?" Ruby asked.

"Why not?" I asked.

"After what she did!"

"I don't understand."

"She was spreading rumours about me. It was you who told me, remember?"

"But Kirsten wouldn't lie about you!"

"But you said she did."

Everything started to fall into place. Jennings had lied about me so that Ruby stopped being my friend. I had to make sure Ruby knew the truth.

"I lied," I said. "Kirsten wasn't spreading rumours."

Ruby's jaw dropped. "But why would you do that? Kirsten was my best friend. Maybe it's *you* I don't want to be friends with."

She walked off, leaving me watching after her ... again. I was sad all day – even when we did Art, I couldn't cheer up. I was stuck being Jennings, and now Ruby hated me.

When I got back after school and saw Lily, I burst into tears again.

"Jennings?" Lily asked, frowning.

"It's me, Kirsten," I wept. "Jennings wouldn't switch back! She said she likes living my life."

"Come on," she said, leading me into her bedroom. She opened her laptop and showed me a page. "I looked on the internet for the Fountain of Wishes and it said you have to count your blessings."

"My what?"

"You have to think about all the things that you like about your life. That's the only way to reverse the switch. You have to list them and put them in the fountain. Here's a paper and pencil to write them down."

I sat at Lily's desk and thought about all the things I'd missed since becoming Jennings.

My blessings

- My mum and dad always have time for me.
- We always go to fun places and on adventures.
- They make lovely food and we always eat together.
- They notice when I'm unhappy and make me feel better.
- They help me with my homework.

Lily nodded enthusiastically when I showed her the list. "We can ask Mum to take us to the museum after school tomorrow."

"I can't wait until then!" I told her. "We have to go now."

"But Mum's busy – she won't take us."

I looked up at Lily. "Then we'll have to find another way."

It turned out not to be all that difficult. As Lily had said, her mum was busy, sitting at the kitchen table with her head in her laptop. But when I explained I needed to go to the museum to do some homework, Mrs Jones agreed to let me and Lily catch the bus there.

We arrived at the Fountain of Wishes as the sun was going down. The coins still glinted at the bottom of the water as I peered into it. Lily stood back a little as I closed my eyes.

"I wish I could have my life back," I whispered. I folded my list and threw it into the fountain.

Lily came over and hugged me. "I'm going to miss you when you go back," she said.

"Jennings is so lucky to have a sister like you," I said.

"You should tell her that," Lily said, raising an eyebrow.

We caught the bus back to the house.

"Can we play a game?" I asked Jennings' mum after our dinner of pasta with tomato sauce.

She looked at me curiously. "Which one?" she asked.

"Ludo?" I suggested. I'd seen the box up on the top of the bookshelf.

"Well, OK – I'll get the board," Jennings' mum said.

"Bad idea – Mum is a sore loser," Lily said, as we sat around the table.

"Cheeky," Mrs Jones said, but she smiled as we set out the pieces.

"This game is rigged," Jennings' mum said after an hour, as she stepped on another of my properties. Her phone buzzed. "Just a moment – " She got up and answered it. "Hello ... yeah, I'll get right on that – " She hung up and turned to us.

"Sorry, guys, but I've got some work to do. We can finish the game tomorrow. It's really your bedtime anyway."

As we went upstairs, Lily turned to me. "Maybe I'll see you around – you know, when you're you again."

"Count on it," I said, grinning.

I climbed into Jennings' bed and stared at the ceiling. Would I be back to me in the morning? I felt a bit sick thinking about it. I closed my eyes and tried not to worry. I'd done all I could.

Chapter 5

When I woke up the next morning, I hardly dared open
my eyes. At first, I squinted just my right eye open a crack.
I saw blue. The blue walls on my bedroom. *My* bedroom.
I was back! I leapt out of bed and ran down the stairs.
Dad was in the kitchen flipping pancakes.

"Dad!" I said, and hugged him.

"Steady on, kiddo," he said, but he smiled down at me.

"I'm home," I said.

"Right," he said, peering at me strangely.

Mum walked into the kitchen rubbing her eyes. I rushed to her and hugged her too.

"It's far too early," she groaned, but then she smiled.

I ate four pancakes, savouring their deliciousness. But as I cleared my plate away, my stomach dropped like a lift. I'd soon see Jennings at school. And Ruby too.

✳ ✳ ✳

I spotted Jennings sitting on a bench, but there was no sign of Ruby.

"You switched us back! But … how?" Jennings asked, looking miserable.

"I just had to think about all the things that make my life great," I said. "And take the list to the fountain and … here we are."

"Well, Ruby doesn't want to be friends with me, thanks to you," Jennings said.

"Whose fault is that? You lied about me – you stole my best friend."

"I just ... wanted what you had," Jennings said. She bit her lip. "Ruby's a great friend, plus you have an amazing family. They do so much stuff with you."

"But you've been to America."

"Why do you keep telling me that? I already know where I've been."

"You shouldn't have told lies about me just so you could be friends with Ruby," I said. "I don't see why we couldn't have all been friends."

Jennings hung her head. "I'm sorry for lying about you, Kirsten. I'm sorry for wanting to stay in your body."

I sat down next to her on the bench. "I understand," I said. "You shouldn't have lied, but maybe I realise why you did."

Jennings gave me a small smile. "I saw your drawings in your room," she said quietly. "You're cool."

"You think I'm cool?"

Jennings nodded.

"What did you do as me?" I asked her.

"Your mum taught me how to sew," she said. "So you'll probably have to keep that up. We went to a Chinese restaurant and did karaoke ... so you'll probably have to do that again too."

My eyes widened. "You sang in front of the whole restaurant?" I asked.

"I'm kidding," she said. "I didn't sing! But your mum and dad did. They were really good!"

Ruby walked over. She narrowed her eyes at Jennings. "Come on, Kirsten," she said to me.

"Wait, Ruby, we've something to tell you," I said. "Something pretty nuts happened. Jennings and I switched bodies. She's been living my life all weekend – and I've been living hers."

"Ha ha," Ruby said, pulling a face. "You think I'm going to believe that?"

"It's the truth! I made a wish at the fountain in the museum to swap places with Jennings, and it came true!" I stared at Ruby. How could I persuade her this wasn't some big joke? "Jennings has a nan that forces her to eat disgusting soup – right, Jennings?"

Jennings laughed. "She made you eat it too?"

I nodded, pulling a face at the memory.

Ruby looked at Jennings. "So that's why you've been so weird – and why you told me the truth? You were Kirsten the whole time?"

"It was me," I said. "But now I'm back in my body – I'm really Kirsten again."

"Okaaaaaaay," Ruby said slowly.

"Why did you believe Jennings about the rumours?" I asked Ruby. "You know I wouldn't tell lies about you."

"You'd just been so distant ... but you're right. I'm sorry. I never should've believed Jennings." Ruby sighed. "Everything's so messed up."

"What if we were all friends?" I asked. "We could start over."

Jennings and Ruby looked at each other.

"Yeah!" Ruby said.

"But no more lies," I said.

Jennings nodded. "Definitely not. I promise."

"So can we come over to yours tonight?" I asked Jennings. "I want to say thanks to Lily, and check on Eddie. Oh, and we might have to play Monopoly – "

Jennings shrugged. "OK!"

The school bell rang. We linked arms and walked inside, grinning.

Kirsten's feelings

envy

panic

delight